CU00801356

THE C
JOURNEY OF BISCUIT
BOY

Life full of magic, joy, and endless possibilities

Hamid Oudi

MyFalcon LTD

This book is lovingly dedicated to my son, Liam, and my niece, Lily.

Your boundless curiosity, unwavering courage, and bright hope light up my life in ways I can hardly express. Watching you both grow brings me immense joy and fills my heart with pride. You remind me daily of the magic that exists in the world and the endless possibilities that lie ahead. As you navigate through life, remember that you have the strength to overcome challenges and the power to pursue your dreams. May you continue to embrace each moment with enthusiasm and chase your aspirations with determination. You are both destined to achieve greatness, and I am honoured to be a part of your journey.

With all my love,

Hamid

CONTENTS

CHAPTER 1: A SWEET TRANSFORMATION

In the small, cozy town of Treatsville, nestled between rolling hills and green fields, there was a little bakery that everyone adored. This bakery, called

"Sweetman's Bakery," was known for its mouthwatering chocolate biscuits. Every day, the shop's sign would gently sway in the breeze, inviting people in. The sweet smell of cocoa, vanilla, and sugar filled the air, and it was impossible to walk by without feeling tempted to stop inside. Families loved gathering at Sweetman's Bakery in the mornings to share tasty treats, stories, and laughter. It wasn't just a bakery; it was a place where the whole town came together, a happy landmark that everyone cherished.

One bright, sunny morning, something very unexpected and magical happened. Mrs. Sweetman, the friendly baker with a big heart, was busy as usual, preparing her famous chocolate biscuits. Her hands were covered in flour, and she hummed a cheerful tune as she mixed and kneaded the dough. Mrs. Sweetman had been baking for years and could make the perfect biscuit with her eyes closed. She always put extra love into her baking, which is why her treats were so special.

As she was shaping the dough into biscuits, she noticed something strange about one particular biscuit. It was a perfectly round, golden-brown biscuit, and it had a beautiful swirl of icing on top. But this biscuit was different from the others. It started to shimmer and sparkle, almost as if it was a hidden treasure. Mrs. Sweetman leaned closer, squinting her eyes to get a better look. To her amazement, the biscuit began to glow even brighter, and then, with a gentle crack, something unbelievable happened. The biscuit slowly cracked open, and in the blink of an eye, it transformed into a tiny newborn baby!

Mrs. Sweetman's mouth dropped open in shock. She couldn't believe what

she was seeing! Right in front of her, this biscuit had turned into a little baby boy with smooth chocolate-brown skin that sparkled, almost as if he was still covered in cocoa powder. He was tiny, but his wide brown eyes were full of wonder and curiosity as he gazed around the bakery, taking in the bright colours, the smell of sugar, and the warmth of the sunlight streaming through the windows.

Mrs. Sweetman's heart pounded as she hurried over to the baby. She dropped her mixing spoon on the counter and carefully picked up the small, chocolate skinned boy, cradling him gently in her arms. "What in the world?" she whispered; her voice shaky with surprise. The baby boy looked up at her, cooing softly, and wiggled his tiny fingers as if he was already trying to explore the world around him.

As Mrs. Sweetman looked at the baby, she felt a wave of love wash over her. He had no parents and no explanation for how he had come into being, but she knew one thing for sure: she was going to take care of him. The baby seemed so vulnerable, and Mrs. Sweetman felt a strong sense of responsibility. She smiled down at him, her heart swelling with affection. "I'll call you Biscuit," she said, deciding that the magical little boy should keep a name that connected him to where he came from.

Mrs. Sweetman had no idea how Biscuit had come to life, but she knew he was special. As she held him in her arms, she couldn't help but wonder what kind of life lay ahead for this tiny chocolate boy. Little did she know that

Biscuit was destined for a life filled with adventure, learning, and discovery. His journey would be one of growth, as he learned to face challenges, make friends, and find out what it meant to be human.

And so, on that sunny morning in Sweetman's Bakery, the story of Biscuit— the little chocolate biscuit boy—began. What started as an ordinary day for Mrs.

Sweetman quickly turned into the beginning of an extraordinary adventure for Biscuit, who would soon experience the world in ways no one could have ever imagined.

'

CHAPTER 2: DISCOVERING THE WORLD

Mrs. Sweetman named the little boy "Biscuit," and from that moment on, his journey through life began, one exciting day after another. As a baby, Biscuit was curious about everything around him, and his early months were filled with exploration. He quickly learned to crawl, scooting around the bakery, following the sweet smells of cakes and pastries. Every corner of the shop seemed like a new world to him, from the shiny countertops to the flour dusted shelves. Biscuit's favourite spots were always near the delicious treats that Mrs. Sweetman baked. He would crawl under the kitchen table, often finding crumbs of pastries to taste. Sometimes, Mrs. Sweetman would discover him sitting there, with his chocolate face covered in sugar and flour, grinning as if he had just uncovered a great treasure.

Rather than getting upset, Mrs. Sweetman would laugh and lift him into her arms. "You've got quite the sweet tooth, don't you?" she'd say, wiping his messy face with a warm towel. To Biscuit, every little crumb and spill was an adventure, and Mrs. Sweetman always encouraged his curiosity.

As Biscuit started to grow, he became fascinated by more than just the bakery — he was curious about the world beyond the windows. Every day, he would
sit by the large window at the front of the bakery, his face pressed up against the glass,

watching the townspeople as they went about their day. He was especially interested in the children who played outside, running, laughing, and chasing after balls. Their joyful giggles filled the air like music, and Biscuit would watch them with wide eyes, eager to understand the fun they were having.

He began to mimic the things he saw, waving at the passing children and babbling happily to himself. Sometimes the children would wave back, and that made Biscuit feel connected to them, even from inside the bakery. Seeing the children run and jump inspired Biscuit to try walking on his own. At first, he was a bit wobbly, his little legs unsure as they tried to hold him up. He'd take a few steps, stumble, and plop down onto the soft bakery floor. But Biscuit didn't give up. Each time he fell, Mrs. Sweetman was there to encourage him. "Keep going, Biscuit! You'll get it!" she'd say with a smile. And with each day, Biscuit grew stronger and more confident, soon taking his first proper steps across the bakery floor.

By the time Biscuit was two years old, his personality had really blossomed.

He was full of energy and loved to play, especially pretending to be just like Mrs. Sweetman. One of his favourite games was playing dress-up in the bakery. Mrs. Sweetman had a large baker's hat and apron, and even though they were far too big for Biscuit, he loved putting them on. The hat would sit lopsided on his head, and the apron dragged behind him like a cape, but none of that mattered to Biscuit. "I'm Chef Biscuit!" he would declare proudly, his face beaming with excitement. He would march around the kitchen, mimicking Mrs. Sweetman's every move, pretending to be a master baker. Mrs. Sweetman loved his enthusiasm and encouraged him to help her with

the baking. She gave him little tasks, like stirring the batter or sprinkling flour on the countertop. Biscuit loved getting his hands dirty, dipping his fingers into the dough, and sometimes sneaking a taste. He would often end up with flour all over his face and hands, but that only made him more eager to learn. "Look, Mrs. Sweetman! I'm baking just like you!" he would exclaim, showing off his work with pride.

One day, something memorable happened while they were preparing for a big town festival. Mrs. Sweetman had been asked to bake a large batch of cookies for the event, and Biscuit was helping as usual. He was stirring a bowl of dough when, in his excitement, he accidentally bumped into a nearby table. A large bowl of colorful sprinkles tipped over and fell to the floor, scattering sprinkles everywhere. The kitchen floor was suddenly covered in a rainbow of tiny, sugary dots.

Biscuit froze, his eyes wide with worry. He looked up at Mrs. Sweetman, expecting her to be upset. But to his surprise, she didn't get angry. Instead, Mrs. Sweetman laughed, her eyes twinkling with amusement. "Well, look at that! It seems we've made a bit of a mess, haven't we?" she said with a warm smile. Relieved, Biscuit joined in her laughter, and together they began cleaning up the sprinkles.

As they were scooping up the sprinkles, an idea sparked in Mrs. Sweetman's mind. "You know what, Biscuit? Every mistake is a chance to create something new," she said thoughtfully. "How about we add these sprinkles to the cookie dough and see what happens?" Biscuit's face lit up with excitement, and they eagerly mixed the sprinkles into the dough. When the cookies came out of the oven, they were not only colourful but also delicious. The townspeople loved the cookies so much that they became a new favourite treat in the bakery, known as "surprise sprinkle cookies."

From that day on, Biscuit learned an important lesson: mistakes weren't something to be afraid of. In fact, sometimes they led to something wonderful.

Mrs. Sweetman's words stuck with him, and he realized that making a mistake wasn't the end of the world—sometimes it was just the beginning of a new adventure.

Biscuit's confidence in the kitchen grew, and so did his love for learning. With every new baking session, he tried new things, always excited to see what would happen next. And through it all, Mrs. Sweetman was there, guiding him, teaching him, and most importantly, encouraging him to keep exploring and having fun. The bakery was not only his home, but also a place where he discovered the joys of life, one sweet moment at a time. And so, Biscuit's journey continued, filled with laughter, love, and the delicious smell of freshly baked treats. He knew that with Mrs. Sweetman by his side, he was ready to face whatever adventures came his way.

CHAPTER 3: THE CHILDHOOD YEARS

Biscuit's early childhood was filled with joy and new adventures. At three years old, Mrs. Sweetman decided it was time for him to join a nearby nursery school. The nursery was a vibrant, bustling place full of laughter and bright colors. Kids ran around, their imaginations turning ordinary objects into exciting worlds. Biscuit, with his warm smile and cheerful giggle, fit right in. He quickly became popular for his playful energy, always ready to jump into any game. He loved building sandcastles in the play yard, trying to make them bigger and taller each time. Finger-painting was another favourite, but being from a bakery, Biscuit would sometimes use icing to create his colourful masterpieces, making everyone laugh. His favourite game, though, was "Super Biscuit." He'd tie an old kitchen towel around his neck like a cape, pretending to save the day from imaginary villains. His friends loved it, cheering as he "flew" around, rescuing them from invisible dangers. But even though Biscuit was always smiling on the outside, there was a little part of him that felt different, a part he didn't talk about. While his friends

played and laughed, Biscuit sometimes wondered why he wasn't like everyone else. In the quiet moments, he'd think, "Why am I not like the other kids? Where did I come from? Why don't I have a family like they do?" These questions made him feel a bit insecure, even if he didn't fully understand why. Whenever his classmates talked about their moms and dads picking them up or tucking them in at night, Biscuit felt a small pang in his chest. It was something he couldn't explain—a strange mix of curiosity and sadness. He loved Mrs. Sweetman dearly, but deep down, he wondered what it would be like to have a family of his own.

By the time he turned five, those feelings grew stronger. The first day of school was exciting, but also scary for Biscuit. He watched as the other kids hugged their parents goodbye, families chatting and laughing together. Biscuit stood there quietly, feeling a bit lost. He didn't have anyone to wave goodbye to, and the sight of all the other kids with their families made his heart ache in a way he didn't understand. Even though Mrs. Sweetman loved him, he couldn't shake the feeling that he was somehow different, and that difference made him feel lonely.

Determined to fit in, Biscuit tried his best to hide his insecurities. He watched his classmates carefully, trying to learn how to act like them. He noticed how they laughed together, how they teased each other, and how they knew when to comfort someone when they were sad. He mimicked their actions, hoping that by doing so, he would blend in. But deep down, he still felt a bit like an outsider. While the other kids seemed so sure of where they came from and who they were, Biscuit was still trying to figure it all out. One day, Biscuit's feelings of loneliness became too much. During recess, he watched a group of kids play with their parents, running and laughing. He felt a lump in his throat as he sat by himself, pretending not to care. "Why don't I have that?" he wondered, his chest tight with emotion. His insecurities felt overwhelming, and for the first time, Biscuit began to doubt himself. "Maybe I don't belong here," he thought.

Then came the school talent show, which brought even more nervousness. Biscuit wanted to fit in, but he also wanted to stand out in a way that made him feel proud. But what could he do? He wasn't sure if anyone would understand his feelings or if they would accept him for who he really was.

The idea of standing in front of his classmates filled him with anxiety. But then, he had an idea. Biscuit realized there was something he was really good at—baking. It was something that always made him feel happy and connected to Mrs. Sweetman. So, for the talent show, he decided to bake a batch of cookies to share with his classmates. As he carefully mixed the dough, he felt a sense of calm wash over him. The familiar process of baking made him feel at ease, and he poured his heart into every cookie. On the day of the talent show, Biscuit stood nervously in front of his classmates, his tray of cookies trembling in his hands. He worried they might laugh at him or not like his idea. But as he passed out the cookies, something magical happened. His classmates smiled and clapped, their eyes lighting up with delight as they tasted the treats he had made. The room filled with applause, and Biscuit felt a warmth spread through his chest—a feeling he had never experienced before. For the first time, Biscuit realized that he didn't need to be exactly like everyone else to fit in. He could connect with others in his own way, through his kindness and creativity.

That moment was life-changing for Biscuit. He saw that he had something special to offer, and that being different didn't mean he didn't belong. While he still wondered about where he came from and what it meant to be human, Biscuit learned an important lesson: the connections we make with others can be just as powerful as the families we're born into. Through his baking and his kindness, Biscuit found a way to be part of something bigger, creating his own sense of belonging, one sweet treat at a time.

CHAPTER 4: THE TEENAGE YEARS

As Biscuit grew older, he went through a lot of changes. He wasn't the playful, round-cheeked little boy he used to be. His cheeks thinned out, and his playful personality became more serious and thoughtful. He was still kind and fun, but now he was facing the confusing world of being a teenager. Biscuit began to wonder about more complicated things, like who he really was, how others saw him, and what his future would look like. But with all this thinking came new worries and insecurities. He no longer saw his unique origins as a fun secret; instead, they became something he felt self-conscious about.

At high school, Biscuit felt like an outsider. While other teens were making friends easily, dating, and fitting into their social groups, Biscuit often felt different. He didn't have the same background or family that his friends had, and that made him feel lonely at times. He would walk through the crowded hallways of his school, watching his classmates chat about their weekend plans or laugh about something silly that happened in class. He longed to feel that same sense of belonging but often found himself questioning where he fit in. Sometimes, he'd look around and think, "Do I really belong here? Do they see me as just like them, or do they think I'm different?" Biscuit also struggled with the pressures of teenage life. While his friends worried about their grades, their looks, or impressing their crushes, Biscuit's worries went deeper. He wasn't just trying to fit in—he was trying to figure out what it meant to be a normal person in a world where he felt anything but normal. This made him feel like he was carrying a weight that no one else understood. Even when he was surrounded by people, he sometimes felt very alone.

But Biscuit had one thing that always made him feel like he belonged—his love for baking. Whenever he felt down, baking helped him focus. The simple act of mixing ingredients, kneading dough, or decorating a cake made everything feel right again. One day, during his sophomore year, Biscuit's teacher noticed his incredible talent for creating delicious and beautiful desserts. She encouraged him to enter a local baking competition. At first, Biscuit wasn't sure. What if he wasn't good enough? What if he failed? He worried about what people would think of him, and the idea of stepping out of his comfort zone was scary. But after some thought, Biscuit decided to go for it. He spent weeks planning and designing a chocolate cake that would stand out. He wanted to make something that not only tasted amazing but also looked like a piece of art. In the end, he created a cake that looked like a mountain, with tiny trees made of chocolate and rivers of blue icing. He poured his heart into every detail, wanting it to be perfect. It wasn't just about winning the competition—it was about proving to himself that he was capable of great things, even when he doubted himself.

When the night of the competition came, Biscuit was a bundle of nerves. The room was filled with bakers of all ages, each presenting their best creations.

There were towering cakes, intricately decorated pies, and colourful cookies. Biscuit's hands shook as he carefully placed his cake on the display table. As the judges walked around, tasting and examining each entry, Biscuit could barely breathe. But when they reached his cake, he saw their eyes light up with surprise and excitement. When they announced that Biscuit had won first place, a wave of pride and relief washed over him. He had done it! For the first time, Biscuit felt like he truly belonged, not because he was trying to fit in, but because he was being himself.

The win gave Biscuit a huge confidence boost, but it also came with new challenges. With every success, Biscuit felt more pressure to live up to expectations. He wanted to fit in with his friends, but he also didn't want to lose the special part of himself that made him who he was. Often, after school, Biscuit would sit by the bakery window, staring out at the world beyond. He would wonder about his future. Would he stay in Treatsville and continue baking with Mrs. Sweetman? Or was there something bigger waiting for him outside the town? These thoughts filled his mind, making him feel both excited and nervous about what lay ahead.

Biscuit's teenage years weren't just about baking competitions, though. Like any teenager, he experienced friendship, crushes, and heartache. In art class, he met a girl named Emily. She was creative, full of energy, and had a spark that drew people to her. Biscuit found himself liking her more and more as they spent time together. They would sit together at lunch, talking about art, baking, and their dreams. Biscuit felt comfortable around her, but at the same time, he was terrified. What if she didn't like him the way he liked her? What if she thought he was strange because of where he came from? Biscuit was filled with doubt, and the fear of being rejected was almost unbearable. He often thought about telling Emily how he felt but was never brave enough to do it. Instead, he kept his feelings to himself, wrestling with the fear of being different. He would daydream about them hanging out after school, maybe even going to a school dance together, but he couldn't find the courage to make it happen. His feelings for Emily were a lesson in vulnerability. He learned that it was hard to open up to people, especially when you were afraid of being hurt. But even though he never told Emily how he felt, the experience taught Biscuit something important—being vulnerable was part of growing up, and sometimes, it was okay to be afraid.

As the years passed, Biscuit continued to learn, grow, and discover who he was. He faced challenges, but he also found victories along the way. Whether it was winning a baking competition or learning to deal with his insecurities, Biscuit realized that being different wasn't a weakness—it was what made him special. Even though he still had moments of doubt, Biscuit knew that he was on a journey to finding himself, and that journey was just beginning.

CHAPTER 5: UNIVERSITY LIFE

As Biscuit finished high school, he was filled with excitement but also a little nervous about starting university. It was a big step, and he knew it would be full of new experiences. He decided to study culinary arts because he wanted to become a great chef and make a name for himself in the baking world. The idea of learning even more about food and baking thrilled him, and he couldn't wait to dive into it.

When he arrived at the university, he was amazed by how lively the campus was. There were students from all around the world, each bringing their unique cultures and personalities. Biscuit felt a rush of energy being surrounded by so many different people. The air was filled with laughter and chatter, and he loved being part of it. Every day felt like an adventure as he met new friends and learned about their lives. He soaked up knowledge from his teachers, who were experienced chefs, and he learned a lot from his classmates, who were also passionate about cooking and baking.

Biscuit's culinary classes were both fun and challenging. He learned to think carefully about flavours, experimenting with sweet and savoury combinations. His instructors encouraged him to be creative and to always think about how to make his dishes look beautiful on the plate. He spent hours in the kitchen, often working late into the night, trying out new recipes and baking techniques. The passion for baking fuelled him, and he couldn't get enough of it!

His dorm room often smelled like a bakery because Biscuit and his classmates loved to bake together. They would gather in the dorm kitchen, where they had all the equipment they needed to whip up late-night snacks. Sometimes they made gooey chocolate chip cookies, other times they baked fluffy cupcakes with colourful frosting. As they worked side by side, they would laugh, share stories, and swap recipes, creating delicious treats and fun memories. Those late-night baking sessions not only filled their bellies but also helped them become lifelong friends.

One of Biscuit's favourite things about university life was the camaraderie he found among his classmates. They all shared a love for food, and this common passion created a special bond. Whenever one of them had a great idea for a recipe, they would gather to try it out. Biscuit loved collaborating with others and was always eager to learn from his peers. They taught each other new techniques and shared their successes and failures, which made their skills grow even faster.

It was during these exciting university years that Biscuit discovered something truly special love. He met a fellow student named Lila, who was just as passionate about baking as he was. She had a bright and cheerful personality that lit up every room she walked into. Her laughter was contagious, and Biscuit felt a warm connection to her. They first bonded over shared recipes, exchanging ideas about cakes and pastries, and quickly became inseparable.

Lila was not only a talented baker but also had a creative spirit. She loved to sketch designs for cakes and dream up new flavours, and Biscuit was inspired by her enthusiasm. They often spent late nights together in the kitchen, trying out new ideas, like a chocolate cake with raspberry filling or cupcakes decorated to look like rainbows. Every creation was a new adventure, and they enjoyed the thrill of experimenting with flavours and decorations. They would also study together in the library, where Biscuit would work on his notes while Lila sketched her cake designs. Biscuit admired her focus and dedication, and he found himself daydreaming about their future together. They supported each other through the ups and downs of university life, cheering each other on during exams and celebrating successes, big and small.

As their friendship blossomed into a sweet romance, Biscuit realized just how much Lila meant to him. They spent countless afternoons walking around the campus, talking about their dreams and what they wanted to achieve after graduation. Biscuit felt so lucky to have someone who understood his passion for baking and shared his dreams. Together, they were not just baking; they were building a life filled with love, creativity, and shared aspirations. In those years, Biscuit learned that love could be just as fulfilling as baking, filling his heart with joy and excitement. As they continued their journey together, he felt more confident than ever. He was growing into the person he wanted to be, and he couldn't wait to see what the future held for him and Lila, hand in hand, exploring all the sweet possibilities ahead.

CHAPTER 6: A LIFE OF LOVE

After Biscuit finished university, he and Lila grew even closer. They spent a lot of time talking about their dreams for the future, and one of their biggest dreams was to open a bakery together. They both loved baking, and they thought it would be amazing to create a special place where people could come together and enjoy delicious treats. With excitement in their hearts, they started planning what their bakery would look like and how it would work. Biscuit and Lila imagined a cozy bakery that smelled wonderful, filled with the scent of fresh pastries, cookies, and cakes. They wanted it to be a place where people could sit and enjoy their treats while chatting with friends or spending time with family. Biscuit dreamed of making all sorts of tasty goodies, while Lila thought about how to design the bakery to make it look inviting and fun. They wanted their bakery to feel warm and welcoming, a little slice of happiness in their town.

They both knew that opening a bakery wouldn't be easy. First, they needed to find the right location. They walked around different neighbourhoods, looking for a spot that would be perfect for their bakery. They pictured it filled with smiling customers enjoying their delicious creations. Each day, they visited different places and wrote down notes about what they liked and didn't like.

Sometimes they felt excited, and other times, they worried if they would ever find the perfect place.

Next, they had to figure out how to pay for everything. Biscuit and Lila talked about getting help from their families or maybe finding a bank that would give them a loan. They worked on their business plans, which included all their ideas for the bakery and how they would make money. They met with a friendly business advisor who gave them tips and helped them understand how to start their own shop.

While they were busy planning, they faced some tough times. Sometimes they doubted whether they could really do it, and that made them feel a little scared. But every time they hit a bump in the road, they remembered how much they loved baking together, and that helped them keep going. They learned that it was okay to face challenges because they could figure things out together. With each problem they solved, they became stronger as a team. One evening, when Biscuit felt ready to take another big step, he decided he wanted to propose to Lila. He wanted to ask her to be his partner for life and in their bakery adventure. Biscuit thought about how special it would be to ask her in the very bakery where he had spent so many happy moments. On a chilly winter evening, he planned a sweet surprise. He decorated the bakery with twinkling fairy lights, making it feel magical and cozy. The wonderful smell of fresh-baked bread filled the air, wrapping them in warmth. When the time came, Biscuit felt a little nervous but mostly excited. He knelt down in front of Lila, holding a ring he had made from chocolate! The ring was decorated with a delicate icing flower that he had crafted himself. It was unique, just like their love. With his heart racing, he looked up at her and said, "Will you be my partner in life and baking?" Lila's eyes sparkled with happiness, and her smile was brighter than the lights around them. Of course, she said yes!

Their wedding was a whimsical and joyful celebration held in the same bakery where they had shared so many memories. They decorated it with soft pastel colors and beautiful flowers that smelled sweet. Friends and family gathered to celebrate their love, filling the bakery with laughter and happiness. Biscuit felt his heart swell with joy as he exchanged vows with Lila, promising to support each other in baking and life.

As they stood together, surrounded by all the people who had watched their journey, Biscuit thought about how far they had come. They had faced challenges, shared dreams, and built a life together filled with love and creativity. Now, as they celebrated their wedding, he knew they were ready for the next exciting chapter in their lives, filled with even more adventures in baking and in love. The future was bright, and together they would make every moment delicious!

CHAPTER 7: A NEW GENERATION

As time went on, Biscuit and Lila's family grew bigger and brighter. They welcomed two beautiful children into their lives: a boy named Charlie and a girl named Bella. Biscuit was so excited to become a father! He loved sharing his passion for baking with his kids and teaching them all the fun things he had learned over the years.

Every weekend, the kitchen turned into a magical playground filled with joy and laughter. Biscuit would gather Charlie and Bella around the big kitchen table, where they would mix batter, roll out dough, and decorate cupcakes with colorful sprinkles. The air would be filled with the sweet smells of chocolate and vanilla, making everyone's mouths water. The kitchen was never quiet; it was always filled with giggles and sometimes even a bit of chaos. They often had flour fights, tossing soft white flour into the air, giggling as it settled on their heads and shoulders, turning them into little powdery bakers.

Biscuit loved telling stories about his own magical beginnings as a chocolate biscuit. He would sit them down and explain how he had once been just a simple treat in a bakery before becoming a loving husband and a caring father. Charlie and Bella listened with wide eyes, fascinated by their dad's incredible journey. Biscuit used these stories to encourage them to embrace their own uniqueness. He would tell them that it was important to be kind, creative, and strong, no matter what challenges they faced.

During their baking sessions, Charlie and Bella often pretended to be master bakers. They would come up with their own ideas for new flavours and even invent their own desserts. One day, while they were all baking together, Charlie accidentally knocked over a big bag of flour, and it spilled everywhere! The flour poofed up like a cloud, covering Bella from head to toe. At first, she was surprised, but then she burst into laughter, and soon, Charlie was laughing too. Biscuit couldn't help but join in the fun, chuckling at the sight of his flour-covered kids. "Sometimes the best recipes come from the messiest moments!" he said with a big grin on his face, feeling so much love for his little bakers.

As Charlie and Bella grew older, Biscuit made sure to fill their lives with adventure and curiosity. He believed that learning was an exciting journey! He would take them on field trips to local farms, where they could see how fresh fruits and vegetables were grown. They would run through fields, pick strawberries, and marvel at the chickens clucking around. Biscuit taught them how important it was to appreciate where their food came from, and they loved every minute of it. They also visited the bustling local markets together, gathering ingredients for their baking experiments. The markets were filled with colourful fruits, fresh bread, and friendly vendors, and Biscuit made sure these outings were fun lessons in exploring the world around them.

Being a parent wasn't always easy, and Biscuit knew that. But he faced every challenge with a patient heart and a smile. Whenever Charlie or Bella had a rough day or felt sad, he was right there to wipe away their tears and give them hugs. He celebrated every little achievement, whether it was learning to ride a bike or finishing a big puzzle. He always reminded them how unique and special they were, making sure they felt loved and supported in everything they did.

Sometimes, when Biscuit reflected on his own childhood, he thought about the importance of love and community. He realized that the greatest gifts he could offer to his children were the lessons he learned growing up. He wanted Charlie and Bella to know that they could always lean on their family and friends, just like he had. Biscuit cherished the moments spent together, knowing that these little adventures and lessons would shape his children into wonderful people.

As they all worked together in the kitchen, played in the bakery, and explored the world outside, Biscuit knew that the love they shared as a family was the most important ingredient in their lives. No matter where life took them, he was proud to be their dad, guiding them through their own magical journey filled with laughter, baking, and love.

CHAPTER 8: THE LEGACY OF BISCUIT BOY

Years went by, and Biscuit couldn't help but feel a warm glow of happiness as he watched his children, Charlie and Bella, grow up. They were becoming wonderful little bakers just like him! Their eyes sparkled with excitement whenever they mixed ingredients together, and they loved creating their own treats. Biscuit felt proud every time he saw them experiment with flavours— Charlie would add a pinch of cinnamon to cookies, while Bella would swirl in bright colours to make cupcakes look like rainbows. It filled his heart with joy to see them carry on his love for baking.

Biscuit and Lila's dream of opening a bakery finally came true! They named it "Biscuit Bliss" as a special tribute to their journey together. Every corner of the bakery was filled with warmth and love, and the delicious smells of fresh pastries made everyone feel happy inside. It was in the heart of Treatsville, where families gathered to enjoy sweet treats and share moments of joy. The bakery quickly became a beloved spot in the town—a symbol of hope, love, and magic.

Every day, Biscuit would take a moment to look around at all the laughter and smiles in his bakery. He knew that life was a series of transformations, like how he transformed from a little chocolate biscuit to a loving husband and father. He often thought about the lessons he learned along the way, like how to face tough times, embrace love, and find joy in even the smallest things. Each day was sweeter than the last, and he felt grateful for every moment he shared with his family.

Biscuit found even more happiness in mentoring young bakers who walked through the doors of Biscuit Bliss. When children came in, their eyes wide with wonder, he would greet them with a big smile. "Welcome to Biscuit Bliss! Let's make something amazing together!" he would say. Biscuit loved encouraging these budding bakers to be creative and adventurous, just like he had been. He reminded them that every mistake was a chance to learn something new. Once, when a young girl accidentally dropped a tray of cookies, Biscuit gently said, "Don't worry! Let's pick them up and turn this into a fun cookie crumble topping for ice cream!" The girl's eyes lit up with joy, and they turned the mishap into something delicious.

With Lila by his side, they organized fun baking classes for kids in the community. The bakery buzzed with excitement as children gathered around, their tiny hands eager to mix, knead, and decorate. Biscuit and Lila showed them how to make cookies that looked like stars and cupcakes topped with fluffy frosting. The room was filled with laughter and the sweet aroma of baking. Each child left with a box of treats and a big smile on their face, and

Biscuit loved seeing the spark of creativity in their eyes.

As Biscuit shared his creations with the community, he realized that the essence of his journey was about connection and inspiration. He often gathered his family around the dinner table after a long day, sharing meals filled with warmth and laughter. The table was always set with delicious food, and they would talk about their day, sharing funny stories and encouraging one another. "Remember, it's important to support each other," Biscuit would say, reminding Charlie and Bella that they were a team. At dinner, they would often talk about their dreams. Charlie wanted to create the biggest cake ever, while Bella dreamed of opening a cupcake shop one day. Biscuit listened with pride, knowing that their aspirations were beautiful reflections of their unique personalities. He encouraged them to chase their dreams, reminding them that it was okay to stumble along the way. "Just like baking, life has its ups and downs," he would say. "But that's what makes it exciting!"

As the years passed, Biscuit watched Charlie and Bella grow into kind-hearted and creative individuals. They would often join him in the bakery, laughing as they worked side by side. Biscuit cherished these moments, knowing that they were building memories together that would last a lifetime. Each day at Biscuit Bliss was a new adventure filled with love, laughter, and endless possibilities. Biscuit knew that no matter where life took them, the values of kindness, creativity, and family would always guide them. Through all the sweet moments and the little challenges, Biscuit found joy in the simple things—baking together, sharing meals, and creating lasting connections with their community. He felt grateful for the love that surrounded him and knew that, just like a perfectly baked cookie, life was

best enjoyed when shared with those you love.

EPILOGUE: A SWEET LEGACY

Biscuit sat in his cozy bakery, surrounded by the sweet aroma of freshly baked cookies, cakes, and pastries. The sun was slowly setting over Treatsville, painting the sky in warm shades of orange and pink. Laughter filled the air as his children, Charlie and Bella, played nearby, their giggles like music to his ears. They were baking cupcakes together, and their flour covered faces were priceless! Biscuit couldn't help but smile, his heart swelling with love and pride.

As he watched them, he remembered his incredible journey—from being a simple chocolate biscuit to becoming a loving father and husband. It felt like a fairy tale full of magic, joy, and endless possibilities.

Biscuit thought about the challenges he faced along the way, how he had once felt lonely and unsure. But each moment, each lesson learned, had led him to this beautiful life filled with love and laughter.

"Look, Daddy! We made a tower of cupcakes!" Charlie shouted; his eyes wide with excitement as he presented their colourful creation. Bella clapped her hands, her face beaming with joy.

"That's amazing, you two!" Biscuit cheered, his heart glowing with happiness. "You're both such talented bakers!" He pulled them close for a big hug, feeling their warmth and energy surround him.

As the sun dipped below the horizon, Biscuit took a deep breath, savouring the sweetness of the moment. He whispered a quiet thank you to the universe for his extraordinary life—a life filled with love, friendship, and delicious treats. Every challenge he faced had shaped him into the father he was today, and every joyful moment made him realize just how special life could be. Years passed, and Biscuit's bakery, "Biscuit Bliss," continued to thrive. It was more than just a place to buy sweets; it was a warm, welcoming haven for everyone in the community. Families gathered there to celebrate birthdays, anniversaries, and special moments. People smiled as they walked through the door, drawn in by the sweet scents wafting through the air. Biscuit loved seeing how happy his bakery made people and how it brought them together.

One day, as Biscuit kneaded dough in the kitchen, a familiar face walked in. It was Mrs. Sweetman, the kind-hearted baker who had first found him as a chocolate biscuit. Her smile brightened the room like sunshine.

"Biscuit! My dear, it's so good to see you!" she exclaimed, wrapping him in a warm hug.

"Mrs. Sweetman! It's wonderful to see you! Thank you for everything you've done for me," he said, his voice full of gratitude.

Mrs. Sweetman smiled and waved her hand, brushing off his thanks.

"Oh, Biscuit! You've created such a beautiful life for yourself. I'm so proud of you!"

Biscuit felt a rush of emotion. He remembered how lost he had felt before meeting her, how her kindness and encouragement had changed his life. "I couldn't have done it without your support,

Mrs. Sweetman. You believed in me when I didn't believe in myself," he said, his voice a little shaky. Tears sparkled in Mrs. Sweetman's eyes.

"You've turned into a wonderful man, Biscuit. And now, look at your children! They're so full of creativity and love.

You've given them the same magic you found in baking."

Biscuit nodded, feeling warmth spread through his heart. He thought of Charlie and Bella, how they were blossoming into incredible young bakers, just like him. They were filled with dreams and ideas, and he couldn't wait to see where life would take them.

As the days turned into weeks, Biscuit and Lila continued to pour their hearts into "Biscuit Bliss." Their children helped with the bakery, eagerly learning how to decorate cakes and whip up delicious treats. Biscuit made it a point to spend time with them every day, sharing his passion for baking while teaching them the importance of hard work, kindness, and creativity. One rainy afternoon, as Biscuit was cleaning up after a busy day at the bakery, he noticed Charlie sitting at the kitchen table, his head resting in his hands. Biscuit's heart sank.

"Charlie, what's wrong?" he asked gently, kneeling beside him.

"I… I don't know if I'm as good as the other kids at baking, Daddy.

They all have fancy ideas, and I feel like I'm just… average," Charlie said, his voice barely above a whisper.

Biscuit felt a wave of empathy wash over him. He remembered his own insecurities as a child.

"Charlie, you are unique and special in your own way. It's not about being better than anyone else; it's about sharing your love for baking. Remember, every great baker starts somewhere. Just keep trying, and don't be afraid to make mistakes. That's how we learn," he reassured him.

Charlie looked up, his eyes shimmering with hope. "Really? You think so?" "I know so!" Biscuit replied, his heart full. "Why don't we bake together and create something new? Let's turn this day around!" He offered his hand, and

Charlie took it, a small smile spreading across his face.

In the warm glow of the bakery, father and son mixed flour, sugar, and a secret ingredient: love. They created a batch of cookies filled with colorful sprinkles, each one a little masterpiece. As they baked, they shared stories and laughter, forgetting all about Charlie's worries. When the cookies came out of the oven, the smell was heavenly.

"Look at those! They're amazing!" Biscuit exclaimed, his eyes wide with pride.

Charlie beamed with joy.

"Thanks, Daddy! I can't wait to share them with

Bella!"

Biscuit knew in that moment that he was not just teaching his children how to bake; he was teaching them how to believe in themselves.

As the seasons changed, Biscuit and Lila watched as Bella and Charlie flourished in their baking skills. One sunny Saturday, Biscuit gathered the family for a special project. "Let's create a new dessert for the bakery's menu! Something that represents all of us!" he suggested.

"Can we make it colourful and fun?" Bella asked, her eyes sparkling.

"Of course! Let's brainstorm ideas together!" Biscuit encouraged. They spent the afternoon sharing ideas, laughing, and sketching designs for their dessert. They decided to create a colourful "Rainbow Delight Cake," with layers of different flavours and a swirl of icing on top.

The next day, they all gathered in the kitchen, ready to bring their creation to life. Biscuit showed them how to carefully layer the cake and decorate it with bright colours. They giggled as they covered each other in flour and frosting, their laughter echoing in the bakery.

When the cake was finally finished, it was a sight to behold! The vibrant layers shone brightly, and the sweet aroma filled the bakery. Biscuit's heart swelled with pride as they stood back to admire their work.

"This is a masterpiece, just like our family!" he declared.

The following week, Biscuit introduced the Rainbow Delight Cake to the customers at the bakery. Everyone loved it! Families came in to share the new treat, and Biscuit felt a warm sense of belonging wash over him. He realized that their love for baking had created a connection between them and the community.

One evening, as the bakery closed and the last customers left with smiles on their faces, Biscuit and Lila sat down together, exhausted but happy. "I'm so proud of our family and everything we've built," Biscuit said, gazing at the glowing bakery.

Lila nodded, her eyes shining with love. "We've created a beautiful life here. Our children are growing into amazing people, and we're sharing our passion with so many others. It feels magical."

Biscuit took a moment to reflect on how far he had come. He thought about the struggles and loneliness he faced as a little chocolate biscuit and how he had transformed into a loving father and husband. He realized that love, patience, and creativity were the true ingredients to a happy life. As the years rolled on, Biscuit watched as Charlie and Bella grew into talented bakers. They had both found their unique paths, inspired by their father's journey. Charlie developed a knack for creating delicious flavours, experimenting with fruits and spices, while Bella blossomed into a brilliant decorator, crafting stunning designs that made their desserts look like pieces

of art.

One sunny afternoon, as the family gathered for a picnic in the park, Biscuit felt a wave of nostalgia wash over him. He looked at his children, their laughter ringing in the air, and he realized just how precious these moments were. He knew that the love they shared would carry them through the ups and downs of life.

Later that evening, as they sat together under a starlit sky, Biscuit gathered everyone around. "I want to tell you something," he began, his voice filled with emotion. "No matter where life takes you, always remember that you can achieve anything if you believe in yourselves and stay true to your passions."

Charlie and Bella listened intently, their faces glowing in the soft light of the stars.

"I was once just a simple chocolate biscuit, and I never imagined I'd become a father, a husband, and the owner of this wonderful bakery," Biscuit continued, his heart full. "But with love and hard work, I've been able to create a beautiful life. You both have the same magic within you."

Tears welled in Lila's eyes as she hugged Biscuit tightly, knowing how much their journey meant to him. "Thank you for always believing in us, Biscuit," she whispered.

As the family shared stories, laughter, and dreams that night, Biscuit felt grateful for the life they had built together. He knew that they were not just a family; they were a team, united by their love for baking and creating joy for others.

Time went on, and as the children grew into young adults, they decided to take on new challenges. Charlie and Bella talked about opening their own bakery locations, inspired by their father's success. Biscuit felt a mixture of pride and a hint of sadness; he knew that his children were ready to spread their wings and create their own paths.

On the day of their bakery openings, Biscuit stood beside them, tears of joy filling his eyes. He watched as they cut the ribbons to their new stores, feeling a sense of fulfilment wash over him. "You've both made me so proud. Remember, no matter where life takes you, I'll always be here cheering you on," he said, hugging them tightly.

As the years rolled on, Biscuit continued to support his children, sharing wisdom and love. He often reflected on his own journey, realizing that life was a series of sweet moments, each one adding to the beautiful story of Biscuit Boy. His heart overflowed with gratitude for the life he had built, surrounded by love, laughter, and a shared passion for baking.

Biscuit spent his days at "Biscuit Bliss," mentoring young bakers who came through the doors. He loved seeing their excitement and creativity as they experimented with flavours and decorations. With Lila by his side, they hosted baking classes, sharing the joy of creating with new generations. Biscuit often gathered the family around the dinner table, enjoying meals filled with laughter, love, and meaningful conversations.

As the sun set on another beautiful day in Treatsville, Biscuit took a moment to reflect. He realized that his journey was not just about baking; it was about love, community, and the joy of sharing happiness with others. And so, the story of Biscuit Boy, the little chocolate biscuit who became so much more, continued to inspire everyone around him. His journey reminded them all that life is sweet, full of possibilities, and meant to be savoured, just like the delicious treats created at "Biscuit Bliss."

The end.

ACKNOWLEDGEMENT

I would like to take a moment to express my heartfelt gratitude to those who have supported me throughout this journey. A special thank you goes to my beloved wife, Maryam. Your unconditional support and love have been my guiding light through every difficulty and challenge. You have stood by me with unwavering strength and encouragement, believing in me even when I struggled to believe in myself. Your patience and understanding have made this journey possible, and I am endlessly grateful to have you by my side. Thank you for inspiring me every day and for being my partner in life and in dreams.

With all my love, Hamid

ABOUT THE AUTHOR

Hamid Oudi, the author of The Curious Journey of Biscuit Boy, immigrated to the UK in 2006 as a child, facing the challenges of adapting to a completely new language, culture, and way of life. Coming from a foreign country with little knowledge of English, Hamid's early years in the UK were filled with both vulnerability and resilience as he navigated school, made new friends, and tried to fit into a world that felt unfamiliar.

Despite the difficulties, he persevered, embracing each challenge as an opportunity to grow.

This personal experience of vulnerability and transformation became the inspiration behind The Curious Journey of Biscuit Boy. In the story, Biscuit, a chocolate treat who transforms into a human, symbolizes the vulnerability Hamid felt as a child trying to find his identity in a new world. Biscuit's journey of growing from a fragile biscuit to a full-fledged human mirrors Hamid's own growth, maturity, and the courage it took to adapt and thrive in a foreign environment.

Hamid's story doesn't stop at personal growth—he went on to carve out a successful career in the tech industry. Over the years, Hamid achieved notable milestones, working with prominent companies and developing a passion for problem-solving, innovation, and leadership. His professional journey is marked by his determination to succeed, despite the uncertainty he faced as a young immigrant.

The Curious Journey of Biscuit Boy is a reflection of the life lessons Hamid has learned along the way—lessons about perseverance, growth, and the strength found in embracing one's uniqueness. Through this magical tale, he hopes to inspire readers of all ages to face life's challenges head-on and discover the sweetness of growth and transformation, just as he has.

Printed in Great Britain
by Amazon

56358515R00046